DREAM BUNNY
... A Rabbit's Tale

The Complete Fable

Written & Illustrated by

CJ Garrett

ReadersMagnet, LLC

Dream Bunny
Copyright © 2022 by Christine Garrett

Published in the United States of America
ISBN   Paperback: 978-1-959165-78-1
ISBN   eBook: 978-1-959165-79-8
ISBN   Hardback: 978-1-959165-86-6
WGA Registration #:   2183516

All rights reserved. No part of this publication may be reproduced, stored in a retrieval system or transmitted in any way by any means, electronic, mechanical, photocopy, recording or otherwise without the prior permission of the author except as provided by USA copyright law.

The opinions expressed by the author are not necessarily those of ReadersMagnet, LLC.

ReadersMagnet, LLC
10620 Treena Street, Suite 230 | San Diego, California, 92131 USA
1.619.354.2643 | www.readersmagnet.com

Book design copyright © 2022 by ReadersMagnet, LLC. All rights reserved.

Cover design by Kent Gabutin
Interior design by Dorothy Lee

All Original Art Paintings by CJ Garrett

Fable of Contents

Dreams Are Real.. 13

Dreams That Sleep 17

Where It Began 18

A Noisy New World 22

Bestest Friend... 25

Not Just A Toy 30

Magical New Land... 33

Back Home 37

Lizzie's Tall Tale.. 39

True Fables 41

Tales Come True 43

Promise Of Adventure 45

Notion Of A Nation 47

Imagine That? 49

Words Come Alive 51

That Happened... 52

Lessons' Learned 54

Bunnies N' More Bunnies.. 56

Anything Is Possible.. 59

Dedicated to the children of the world who will be inspired by their own imagination and share their stories with others.

I am deeply grateful for and offer heartfelt
thanks to all my family, friends, and colleagues
who helped make this book a perfect dream come true.

SPECIAL THANKS TO:
Cynthia Speer, Mikayla Gluskin, Taylor Schuler,
Hal Havins, Maahra Hill, Nikolaj Gluskin, Sylvia Lozano;
her Children & Grand-Children, Christopher & Nicole Welsh
with Brooklyn & Mason, Linda Grenchanuck,
Margaret Tiefenthaler, Kathy Outland, Denis de Boisblanc,
Alemaya Cole, Joan Leighton, William Bradford II,
Donnie Robinson, Sulma Mendosa & her girls.

In Loving Memory
My Parents - Garrett & Frieda Jones,
My Sister - Susan Margarette Havins &
Dear Friend Annelore Stern

Based on the DREAM BUNNY'S TALE SERIES
presented from Screenplay to Television
and our Developing Toy Division

DREAMS are REAL

Mary Lancaster lives at the end of a cul-de-sac in a suburban neighborhood in a California mountain village. There she lives with her three children and her husband Daniel, who travels frequently abroad for work. They all enjoy the gentle seasons the area has to offer and ice skating on the frozen pond.

She also loves to drive through the snow covered streets, lined with quaint little homes and large pine trees; the smell in the air is invigorating. On this day, Mary slowly pulled up in front of their small home which has a wrap- around front porch and a large picture window.

The children cheered as they slowly drove up to the curb to stop. The front porch furniture was covered for the winter and the porch light glowed, welcoming the family back home.

As the car finally came to a full stop, the car door flew open and out charged nine year old Alex, and eight year old Anna. Alex the eldest was short for his age and growing fast, causing him to be clumsy at times, however he always feels he's in charge.

Anna, on the other hand, tall for her age, was graceful, a bit of a know-it-all and a little bit too bossy. Both siblings arrived at the front door at the same time, but somehow Anna managed to grab the keys from under the door mat, opening the door and then ran quickly into the house.

Now the third child, four year old Lizzie, precocious and independent, impatiently wiggled in her car seat, awaiting to be released, so she could catch up with her brother and sister. Mother walked around to Lizzie's door and called out, "Be patient little one! Oh my goodness." Mary smiled to herself, showing her large dimples as she rushed to open Lizzie's car door. She always has humor and love towards her children no matter what the situation.

The family moved to the states before Alex was born and Mary and her husband Daniel, a professor of English history, met in one of his lectures over twelve years ago. Finding a position in America and living in an area with four seasons was a dream come true. Daniel was away giving a lecture in Spain and would be home before the holidays. Mary had a lot more work but did not mind because she loved extra time with her children.

Lizzie continued to fuss as Mary made her way to release her from her confinement. Lizzie called out, "Hurry Marmie or they'll never give me a chance to play." The children called their mother Marmie because when Lizzie was around two years old, she heard her father call her Mary and her sister Anna called her Mummie; so they all giggled when tongue-twisted Lizzie called their mother Marmie and it became her beloved pet name. Lizzie was finally released from her car seat and Marmie headed for the trunk to get the groceries. Lizzie charged towards the front door, then suddenly stopped in mid walkway and looked up into the sky transfixed. Snowflakes hit her eyelashes as she blinked. She looked dazed through the snow and clouds and held her mittens towards the sky. "Marmie, look the snow has lots of colors." She stared at flashes of colors high in the snowy sky. She pointed up, "can't you see it Marmie?" Mary struggled with the bags. "Oh my, I thought you were in a mad dash to get inside?" Lizzie moaned, "but Marmie." She took Lizzie's hand, "come along little day dreamer." Lizzie strained to get a better look up into the sky. "But Marmie I'm not dreaming."

DREAMS that SLEEP

This was not Lizzie's imagination because high above the clouds were indeed rainbow colored lights, sparkling stars, and twinkling musical notes all dancing in a far distant magical kingdom. This place not seen with the naked eye is located beyond our imagination and yet closer than a whisper.

This was the night it all began with night rainbows, colorful clouds, sparkling stars and musical notes. It is a magical place hidden tightly between sleep and the twilight of our dreams. Nestled in all the colorful clouds were thousands of toys, toys and more toys from all generations since time began. As they slept contently in this wonderful place, they smiled thinking about their playmates who were their very best friends growing up. The toys slept and dreamed about days gone by and the love they felt from the children who cared for and played with them. In their dreams they remembered the funny stories their children told them. They all laughed together for hours.

 Watching over this magical place is a special chosen guardian. Not exactly what you might visualize as a protector of such a massive place, but instead he is a sweet loveable brown and white whimsical rabbit named Dream Bunny. With a style all his own he has extraordinary long ears and wears a soft blue nightcap, speckled with white moonbeams. He guards and looks over this enchanted place with the help from his best friend, a little star, named Twinkley.

All dreams float through the sky as we sleep but magic starts when our dreams reach their distant destination, creating this wonderful place. A very careful observer might just be able to see each wish, dream and hope transform into delightful harmonious musical notes, swirling rainbows and the most glorious stars.
BREATHTAKING!

WHERE it BEGAN

Lizzie did see something high up in the snowy sky that night and sensed the magic even though she was too young to know what that was.

What happened that very night, in this magical kingdom, high in the sky, beyond what the eye could see was a content Dream Bunny and Twinkley sleeping, as always. But something had changed, even though it seemed like any other night; stars twinkled, musical notes sang, swirling rainbows danced in the sky, and thousands of toys all nuzzled in colorful clouds slept contentedly.

Then Twinkley awoke and swiftly flew up to Dream Bunny's nose, and twinkled loudly, "Dream Bunny, please awaken!" On this particular night, Twinkley felt troubled. She was concerned because as she looked around, she could see that her fellow stars were losing their sparkle. Although Twinkley had never seen this happen before, she knew that the stars only dim their light when they know there's trouble in the air. This magical place of dreams was losing its joy. With a deep feeling of concern, she looked around at all the toys who were sleeping peacefully on their cozy clouds and wondered, "Will these things cause them to disappear?" After thinking of what to do, she suddenly felt motivated to get Dream Bunny's attention for help. She had to wake him up! She thought she might be able to do that by using her beautiful musical voice while flashing brightly her glistening sparkles. That did not work. So she flickered and flashed as bright as she could. Then sang loudly, "Wake up Dream Bunny, wake up! Wake up, Wake up! Wake up, Dream Bunny, wake up! Wake! Up! Dream Bunny! Wake! Wake! Wake! Up!." Sadly that also didn't work.

Dream Bunny was so content on his mini-moon he never moved or opened a single eye; he simply rolled over and landed comfortably on to a colorful fluffy cloud and fell into a deeper sleep.

Out of frustration, Twinkley sang out to the other stars for help, but even with all of the songs sung by the stars, Dream Bunny just contentedly continued to sleep; it was as if the music lulled him into a deeper quiet slumber. Twinkley then came up with a brilliant idea and called out to all the other stars, "Shhhh, let's be really quiet." It wasn't too much longer before the sound of silence interrupted Dream Bunny's dream; he could no longer stay asleep. Dream Bunny yawned, blinked his eyes open, and called out franticly, "What's going on? Twinkley!--Twinkley? Twinkley! Why is it so quiet? Where are you? Why is it so dark? I feel like something dreadful is happening, Twinkley! Everything seems to be vanishing! Is our magical place disappearing?! Oh my goodness, if that's true whatever shall we do?!" It was at that moment Dream Bunny realized their kingdom was fading away.

As Dream Bunny looked around he couldn't see Twinkley until she finally appeared right in front of his nose and said, "Don't worry Dream Bunny, it's going to be all bright!" Dream Bunny wailed, "How can you be sure Twinkley? This has never, ever happened before." Twinkley sparkled in delight, "Really, it will be all bright? Because I just had the most wonderful flicker of an idea! We must go and see the children who dream and find out what happened." Dream Bunny stopped wailing instantly, looked at Twinkley with an eyebrow raised in puzzlement and said, "That's impossible! It's never been done before; how would we make that happen?!" Twinkley looked back with a twinkling glow and then with a SUDDEN bright FLASH, THEY WERE GONE . . . Twinkley and Dream Bunny simply disappeared!!!

A NOISY new WORLD

In what only seemed like seconds later Dream Bunny found himself in a strange new landscape. He blinked his eyes rapidly and then slowly looked around. His nose twitched with excitement as a wonderful new smell came from a huge plant in front of him. It was nothing like the rainbow flowers in his kingdom of dreams.

As Dream Bunny looked around he flinched with surprise, when a sparkling Twinkley happily appeared in front of his nose as her bright happy self. "That's a pine tree, isn't it fantastic?!" Dream Bunny slowly nodded yes, as he started to reach up to adjust his most adored nightcap; it was gone! Panicked, Dream Bunny patted the top of his head and in its place was a pair of very very long, REAL, furry rabbit ears. "Good grief, what is going on?!"

It was at that moment Dream Bunny realized he could no longer speak! An extremely happy and excited Twinkley soared all around him proclaiming, "Aren't your ears beautiful Dream Bunny? You know, to be in the real world, you have to be a real rabbit. Of course, no one will be able to understand your thoughts, except me." Dream Bunny took his very real paws and covered his eyes in frustration. Thinking loudly, "Twinkley what have you done?" Twinkley flew up to his nose. "Listen - I think I hear children laughing. I wonder if it is coming from that little home over there." Twinkley promptly flew off to take a look.

Dream Bunny sat quietly next to the pine tree as he watched Twinkley fly over to the house. He thought, as loud as he could, "Hey! Since I can't talk, I hope you have a plan so I can chat with the children, if indeed there are children over there. Maybe I should hum to get their attention!?" Once more Dream Bunny thought as loud as he could. "Oh that's right, no one can hear me! Twinkley, you do know I'm annoyed." Frustrated, Dream Bunny decided to follow Twinkley and placed one paw onto the

white ground and jumped. "YIKES, this cloud is freezing cold!" Then Dream Bunny looked up to the sky and called out, "Twinkley there are tiny bits of cold clouds falling apart all over me. It's making my nose cold!" Dream Bunny's nose twitched as he shook his head and snow flew all over the place. "What ARE these tiny cold clouds?"

Twinkley returned and sparkled close up to Dream Bunny. "Those aren't clouds Silly. Its snow and those little bits falling through the air are called snowflakes!" Dream Bunny shook his head and hopped as fast as he could toward the little house. "Whatever it is Twinkley, I don't like it — my toes also feel funny!" Twinkley laughed playfully next to his friend's ear, "I wish you could fly. . . be careful; don't fall, the snow is quite slippery!"

Dream Bunny looked sideways at Twinkley, distracted and irritated. He then tripped on his right ear causing him to somersault in the air. He landed flat on his back in the snow. Twinkley flew over quickly to make sure he was okay. He lie there motionless staring into the sky as snowflakes continued falling all over him. Dream Bunny looked up at Twinkley with frustration. All Twinkley could do is laugh uncontrollably. She almost exploded into a million sparkles.

Dream Bunny got up slowly and grumbled every second. The pair finally reached the steps that led up to the porch. A relieved rabbit hopped right up the steps and headed straight for the window to look inside. He rubbed his toes briskly to warm them up, and sighed, "Snow is cold and slippery — what good is it?"

BESTEST FRIEND

Dream Bunny and Twinkley were very excited and nervous at the same time, but knew they had to stay as silent as they could, so they slowly peered through the window. Once focused, their eyes were drawn to the other side of the room. In the distance, they saw a little girl who stood in the doorway.

The two stared as the little girl with light brown curly hair stood almost three feet tall wearing white pajamas with red polka dots. As she walked towards the window, the two ducked down but heard a voice come from the other room, "Lizzie, are you warm enough? Do you need your robe?" The little girl answered, "No Marmie I'm okay?" Lizzie continued to skip across the room just before she jumped on the padded window seat right in front of the window. She deliberately fogged the window with her breath and drew a happy-face on the glass. During the time Lizzie was totally unaware, two visitors hidden in plain sight outside the window followed her every move.

Dream Bunny and Twinkley watched intently as the Lizzie gazed out the bay window, pressing her nose against the window and sighed, "Isn't snow beautiful?" As Lizzie looked outside she suddenly noticed a slight movement on the porch. She peered through the mist on the window, and blinked her eyes to be certain that it wasn't her imagination working overtime. Sure enough, outside, there stood below the window a rabbit with enormously long ears, and a tiny star hovering brightly by his left ear. Both of them looked up at her. Lizzie turned her head slowly towards the direction of where her siblings were playing, and called out, "You guys!" They ignored her cries and continued playing their video game. Lizzie decided to get louder. "Quick! Come see what I see!" Neither her brother, Alex, nor her sister, Anna, responded ... they were far too involved with their game.

Dream Bunny decided to stand on his tiptoes to make himself taller, and get as close to the window as he could. When he saw

Lizzie SCREAMED, "There's a monster rabbit on the porch, and he's growling at me!! There's also a star twinkling next to him!" Lizzie yelled to her siblings, "C'mon, you guys, I'm not kidding! Go on the porch; I'll prove it!" Their Mother, called from upstairs, "Children please, be less noisy."

With that loud scream from Lizzie, the two friends scrambled across the porch and hid under a wicker chair. Twinkley peeked out from behind Dream Bunny's ear. "What did you do?", Twinkley asked. Dream Bunny quivered and answered, "I just smiled." As they both continued to shake, Twinkley responded, "Well don't EVER do that again!"

Lizzie ran into where her siblings were playing video games and jumped up and down in front of the television screen, blocking it. Alex shouted, "Lizzie get out of the way!" Anna also yelled impatiently, "No way are we going out in the freezing cold on another one of your wild goose chases, Lizzie!" Lizzie insisted, "There aren't any gooses out there, silly, just a monster rabbit and a star!"

Both completely disregarded her pleas, and turned their attention back to the game. Anna and Alex shrieked, screamed and laughed excitedly as Anna won again.

Outside on the porch, Dream Bunny's fur stood straight up out of sheer fright as he grumbled to his equally terrified friend hovering by his side. "Honestly Twinkley, you would think in this real world it would be possible to have ears a little shorter, especially on a real rabbit; and children a bit less frightening! Are you sure this is all part of your plan?" he asked befuddled. He tried to sit up as straight as the cramped hiding place would allow. Dream Bunny became more irritated by the second. Twinkley continued to sparkle. "I love your ears, they're very unique." She quietly chuckled, and got closer to Dream Bunny. She was very relieved to be hidden safely from whatever dangers might be inside that house.

Both sat still as Twinkley sparkled and reflected on all that had happened since their arrival in this new and very different land. Then, her bright spark got larger, indicating she had a brilliant flash of an idea.

Twinkley's bright light surrounded Dream Bunny with rainbows and stars. Twinkley then whispered excitedly, "Dream Bunny, I've got it. I have a plan that will help us in this real world! I know exactly what we need to do!" Gently, Twinkley touched her friends nose. . .instantly transforming Dream Bunny back into a stuffed toy; his magical nightcap reappearing, with Twinkley dangling at the tip of his cap.

Dream Bunny sighed, "Oh, this is a much better plan. Thank you Twinkley, I feel so much more like myself. Wait a minute, I still can't talk. I'm Dream Bunny — I'm supposed to TALK!" Twinkley giggled, "Now don't be a Grumpy Bunny!"

Abruptly, both friends bounced up from the ground as the front door forcibly slammed with a loud BANG. Lizzie stepped out and tiptoed around the front porch. "Ah ha!" she exclaimed, scooping up Dream Bunny into her arms, "Gotcha!" Surprised, as she held him up to the light, "Wait. . . you're not real. You're a toy! And would you look at those ears; they're even longer than I thought!" Lizzie examined the stuffed rabbit, and then tucked him firmly under her arm as she ran back inside. She ran straight upstairs to her room. She leaped upon her bed, and grasped her newfound toy by his ears, swinging him, back and forth, up and down, and to and fro. Dream Bunny groaned while Twinkley on the other hand, jingled happily from the end of Dream Bunny's nightcap, thoroughly enjoying herself.

Lizzie stopped jumping, "What was that sound?" she looked around. Seeing nothing, she shrugged her shoulders in dismissal and continued to swing Dream Bunny as high as she could and then happily declared, "You are the cutest bunny ever, and you are going to be my bestest friend!" Catching sight of the little star dangling at the end of Dream Bunny's nightcap, she shook the little star vigorously. "Was that you jingling?" she exclaimed, and shook the star once more for good measure. Dream Bunny giggled at Twinkley and said, "Having fun yet?" Twinkley chimed, "UUUUGGGGGGGHHHHH." Lizzie stopped again and whispered, "I heard that!"

NOT just a TOY

Lizzie took a moment and looked intently into Dream Bunny's eyes and gave him a kiss on his nose. A very happy Dream Bunny gazed at his new friend and thought how wonderful things were going to be. Without warning, the door burst open. Anna and Alex stormed into Lizzie's room, yelling in unison, "YAAAAHHH!" Lizzie screamed, a terrified Twinkley chimed madly, and poor Dream Bunny could feel his stuffed paws tremble with fright! "You guys! You scared the dickens out of me and my bunny!" Lizzie exclaimed.

Glancing over at Twinkley, Dream Bunny shuddered, "I can't take much more of this!" Just then, all three children burst out laughing and Dream Bunny was silently relieved. Twinkley sighed, "See? It's okay, they were just having fun." Holding Dream Bunny aloft, Lizzie proudly displayed him to her brother and sister, "See what I found, guys?! Didn't I tell you that there was a bunny on the porch?" Alex shook his head and said, "Kiddo, I hate to be the one to break the news to ya, but . . . it's a toy! It's not real! And that star you were going on about — it's hanging at the end of his cap." Anna looked over at Dream Bunny. "Well, he might only be a toy but you have to admit, Alex, he's a really cute one." As she kissed his nose she suddenly paused, "Hey, what was that sound?" A wide-eyed Lizzie exclaimed, "You heard it too!?" The room was silent as all three children strained to hear. Nothing. "Hah! Hah! Hah! You nearly had me, Little Sis', you really did," Alex laughed as he raced out of the bedroom shouting to Anna, "C'mon don't fall for her pranking us."

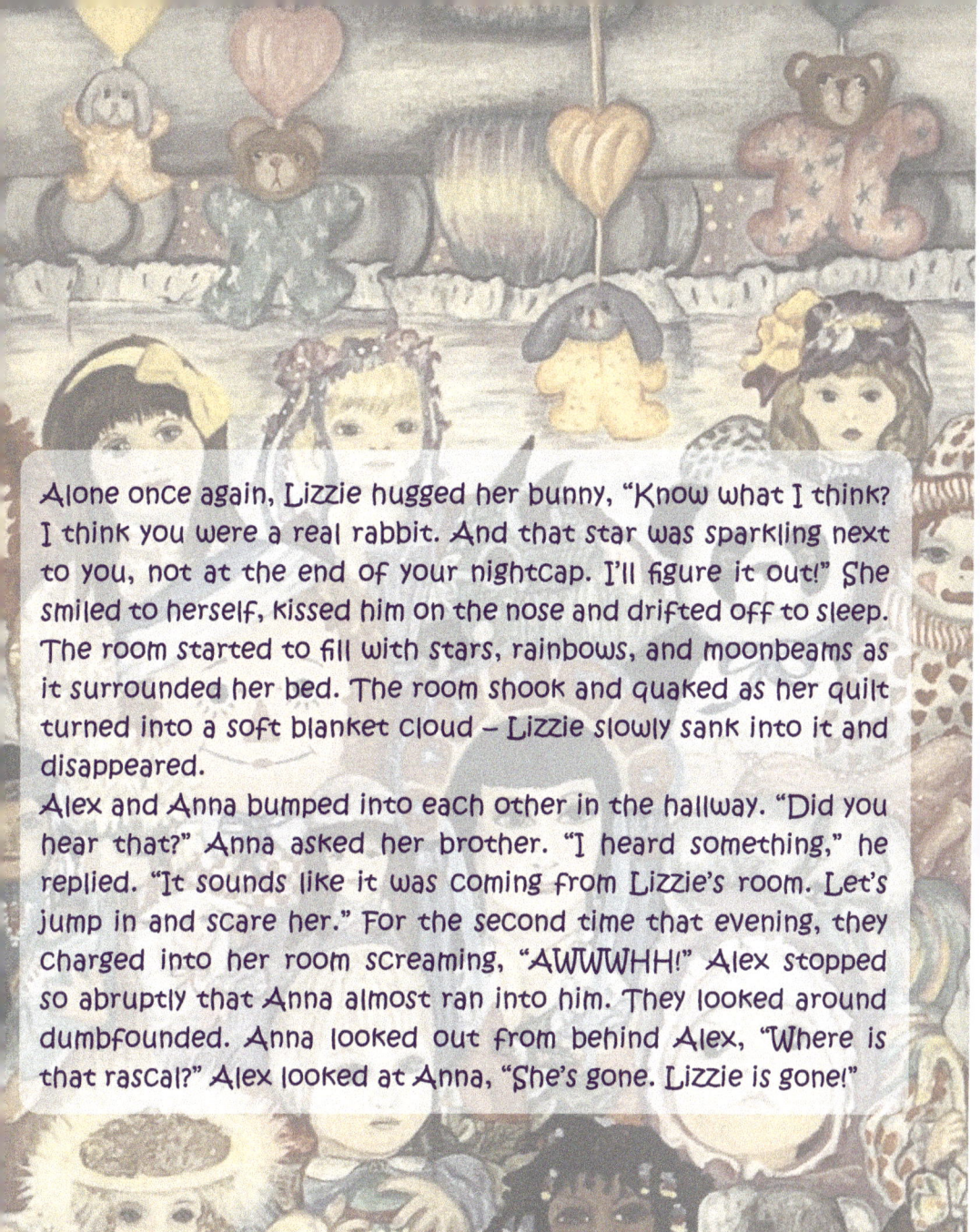

Alone once again, Lizzie hugged her bunny, "Know what I think? I think you were a real rabbit. And that star was sparkling next to you, not at the end of your nightcap. I'll figure it out!" She smiled to herself, kissed him on the nose and drifted off to sleep. The room started to fill with stars, rainbows, and moonbeams as it surrounded her bed. The room shook and quaked as her quilt turned into a soft blanket cloud – Lizzie slowly sank into it and disappeared.

Alex and Anna bumped into each other in the hallway. "Did you hear that?" Anna asked her brother. "I heard something," he replied. "It sounds like it was coming from Lizzie's room. Let's jump in and scare her." For the second time that evening, they charged into her room screaming, "AWWWHH!" Alex stopped so abruptly that Anna almost ran into him. They looked around dumbfounded. Anna looked out from behind Alex, "Where is that rascal?" Alex looked at Anna, "She's gone. Lizzie is gone!"

MAGICAL new LAND

Lizzie sank into her blanket, disappeared and fell in slow motion through an open sky filled with swirling rainbows, thousands of twinkling stars, and many musical notes. Her eyes were wide open and she clutched tightly to her new found bunny. She whispered to him, "What's happening?" As she looked around in amazement she touched one of the notes and the note sang back at her. Shocked in amazement, she dropped her bunny. She franticly tried to grab him in mid air, but missed and tumbled through the air. Then suddenly she landed on a rainbow slide and quickly bounced on the biggest and fluffiest pink cloud she could have ever imagined.

She looked around slowly. "Where am I?" She asked no one in particular. Almost immediately, Dream Bunny popped out from beneath another cloud, and Twinkley flew off the end of his magical nightcap and hovered next to his ear. "We are so glad you're here in our magical kingdom. I'm Twinkley and that's Dream Bunny." Lizzie exclaimed, "I can understand you!" Dream Bunny answered, "As long as you are here with us, you will be able to understand everything. Then, when you wake up in your real world, you can tell other children about us." Twinkley flew up to Lizzie, "That's why you're here. Children need to dream and wish about beautiful things." Dream Bunny added, "And not scream so much." They all laughed. Dream Bunny hopped on a cloud next to Lizzie, "Sadly, hopes, dreams and wishes from children have disappeared and caused our kingdom to fade away." Twinkley chimed in, "By coming here to our magical kingdom from the real world, the hopes, dreams and wishes of all the children in the world will awaken, making anything possible." Lizzie looked seriously into Dream Bunny's eyes and said, "I made that all happen by coming here?"

Then suddenly from behind the clouds Lizzie heard a voice. "You made that possible for us; our hopes, dreams and wishes woke us up." When Dream Bunny heard the voice he was equally surprised;

so much so that he tumbled backward and fell onto another cloud. Twinkley flew over to him and twinkled loudly, "Isn't it brilliant! Everyone woke up!" Dream Bunny shook his head back and forth and asked, "How?" Twinkley happily twinkled. "Well, when Lizzie entered their dreams here, the toys woke up!" Lizzie exclaimed, "I did that!?"

In the distance music echoed, plus sounds of giggling toys. Twinkling stars were seen sparkling brightly from everywhere and musical notes sang loudly. Many toys jumped out to meet Lizzie and danced happily around her. They cheered, "Lizzie you made everything possible!"

Sleepy from all the excitement, Lizzie sat down on a cloud next to a colorful Harlequin Doll who stepped out from behind a beautiful blue cloud. He wore a purple and red outfit and a large hat with tassels. Lizzie asked him, "Where did you come from? What's your name? Have you always lived here?" Harlequin Doll giggled, "My name is Quinlyn. Like all of us, we all lived in your real world until we either got too old or were no longer played with by the children we lived with. When that happened, we simply appeared here in the kingdom of dreams. We would dream about our time with our little friends and about days gone by; but since you came into our dreams, we happily woke up!" Lizzie was so excited, "What do you remember?" Quinlyn smiled and replied, "Hundreds of years ago, I lived with a family and the child who cared for me grew up to be a famous artist who could paint anything that you could imagine. I sat for hours and watched him paint. He even painted me once."

Then from behind yet another cloud, popped out a happy dancing bear. She wore pink and violet topped with a white tulle skirt. Lizzie clapped and laughed. "I'm having the best time ever!" Dancing Bear stood on her toes and leaped across one cloud to the next. "I'm Daphne the Dancing Bear! I lived with a dancer. She was wonderful and I learned everything from her." Lizzie sighed, "Wow, I wish I knew how to paint and dance." Quinlyn smiled at Lizzie, and replied, "Ah, but you can; you can do anything here in our kingdom!"

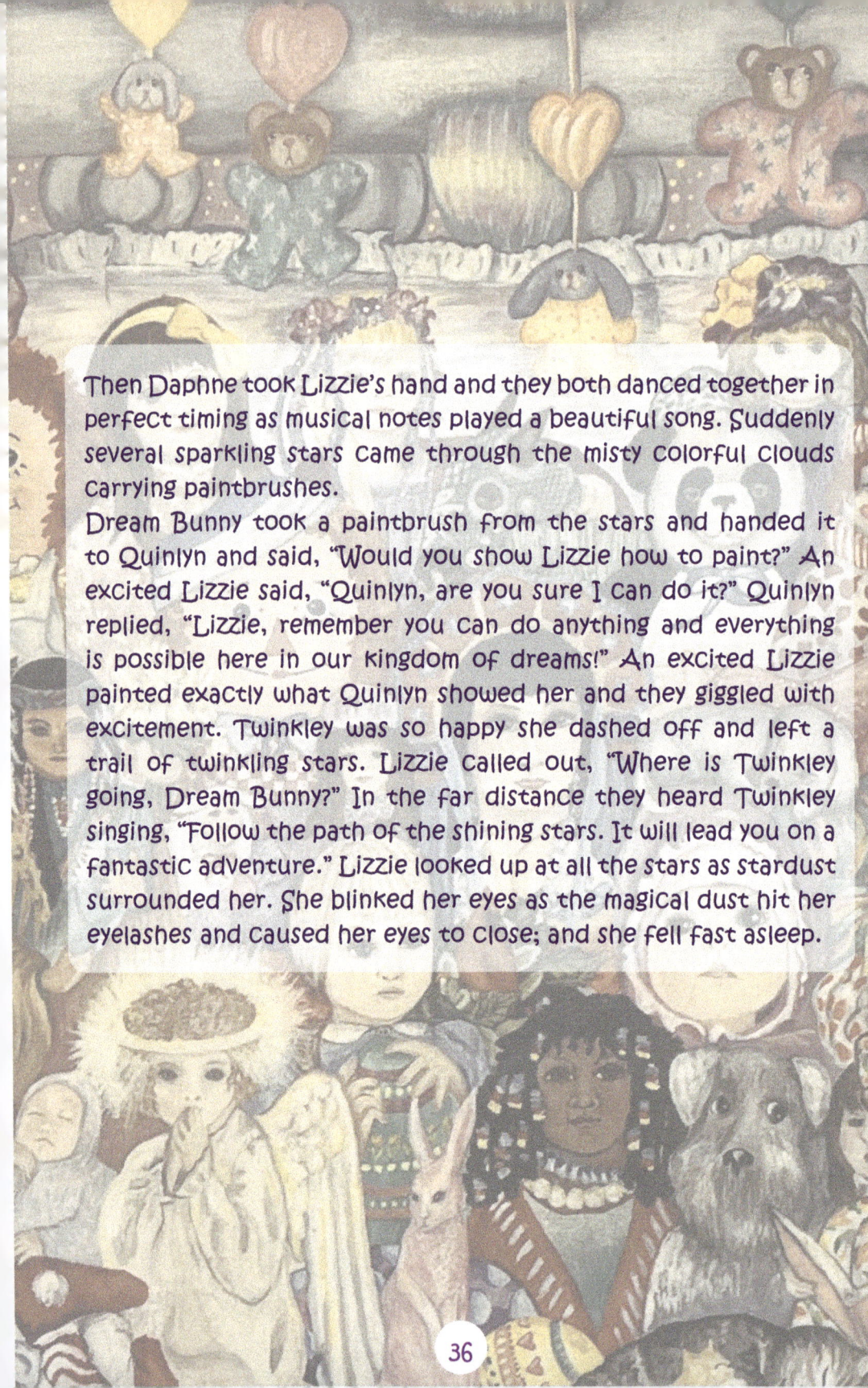

Then Daphne took Lizzie's hand and they both danced together in perfect timing as musical notes played a beautiful song. Suddenly several sparkling stars came through the misty colorful clouds carrying paintbrushes.

Dream Bunny took a paintbrush from the stars and handed it to Quinlyn and said, "Would you show Lizzie how to paint?" An excited Lizzie said, "Quinlyn, are you sure I can do it?" Quinlyn replied, "Lizzie, remember you can do anything and everything is possible here in our kingdom of dreams!" An excited Lizzie painted exactly what Quinlyn showed her and they giggled with excitement. Twinkley was so happy she dashed off and left a trail of twinkling stars. Lizzie called out, "Where is Twinkley going, Dream Bunny?" In the far distance they heard Twinkley singing, "Follow the path of the shining stars. It will lead you on a fantastic adventure." Lizzie looked up at all the stars as stardust surrounded her. She blinked her eyes as the magical dust hit her eyelashes and caused her eyes to close; and she fell fast asleep.

BACK HOME

As the morning light hit Lizzie's face she quickly blinked her eyes and woke up. Lizzie smiled and hugged Dream Bunny, "yippee, let's get breakfast." She then ran downstairs with him tucked under her arm. Once in the kitchen she ran to give her Mother a hug. "Well good morning my little bug." Then there was a thunder of footsteps as Anna and Alex barged through to the kitchen door. Mother turned around, "Well good morning noisy ones." In unison they said, "Good morning Marmie!" They stared at Lizzie as they both walked in and sat down. Lizzie ignored them and spoke to Dream Bunny. "I can't wait until tonight. . .," then she noticed her siblings staring at her. "What?" both Anna and Alex moved their chairs closer to Lizzie. Alex leaned in, "Where were you last night?" Anna piped in, "Yeah we heard noises?" Lizzie looked at both of them in frustration. "I was with Dream Bunny in the kingdom of dreams."

Mother came back to the table and placed plates of French toast in front of all three children. In unison, they all said, "Thank you Marmie." As she placed breakfast in front of Lizzie she noticed Dream Bunny and asked, "Where did that cute little bunny come from Sweetheart?" Lizzie paused and looked over at her brother and sister. "Who? Oh Dream Bunny? He came from the kingdom of dreams with his very most bestest friend, Twinkley, who's a star - but she's not in the real world right now. We have to find her next time ..." Mother smiled fondly at Lizzie, "Such a big imagination, how wonderful." Alex snickered. Mother scolded, "Shush."

Anna and Alex exchanged looks. Mother left the kitchen, then called back, "Don't dawdle. Be ready to leave in twenty minutes." Once Mother was out of site, Alex blurted out, "Okay Lizzie, where were you last night? Where were you hiding?" Lizzie answered, "I wasn't hiding. I went with Dream Bunny to his dream kingdom." All of a sudden Anna wailed, "Oh no, I can't find my green paint, and I need it to color the leaves on my tree."

I'll never finish my homework now!" Lizzie calmly asked her, "Do you have yellow?" Anna answered impatiently, "Yes, I have yellow, but the leaves are supposed to be green." Lizzie persisted, "What about blue? Do you have blue?" Annoyed, Anna answered sharply, "Yes, I have blue. What is your point, Lizzie?" Anna said as Lizzie went back to eating her French toast and replied "Yellow and blue mixed together makes green." Everyone at the table fell silent, and stared in bewilderment at Lizzie. Mother entered the kitchen and overheard Lizzie. "Oh my goodness, where in the world did you learn that Miss Lizzie?" Mother looked over at Anna with approval. "Give it a try." Anna poured a dab of yellow followed by a dab of blue, mixed the two together, and lo and behold she had the perfect green!

Mother looked at the clock. "My goodness we're running late." The doorbell rang. "That's Sulma." Mother took another gulp of tea. "C'mon let's go children."

Lizzie jumped off the chair, spinning the perfect pirouette. "Learned that also, in my make-believe place." She said with an attitude.

Anna and Alex looked at each other dumbfounded. Anna ran quickly out of the kitchen. Alex chased after her and tripped over his own feet. Anna looked back, "C'mon stop goofing around."

Mother opened the front door. "Good morning Sulma." Lizzie ran over to Sulma, giving her a big hug before she could get through the door.

LIZZIE'S tall TALE

Lizzie sat on the big chair in the living room as Sulma vacuumed. Sulma, their family friend, had taken care of all three children since they moved to the states. Sulma dusted while she listened to Lizzie's tall tales. She laughed and said, "Miss Lizzie it's so nice to see you so happy." Lizzie smiled and said, "Dream Bunny makes me happy. We just have to find Twinkley on my next dream visit. You'll meet her when I find her. She's a little star." Sulma enjoyed Lizzie's stories and laughed out loud quite often. As Lizzie sat in the big chair in the living room she cuddled Dream Bunny then suddenly closed her eyes and fell asleep. Sulma quietly walked over and covered her with a soft throw. "You two take a nice nap."

Sulma went to finish her work and a little time later Lizzie woke up and giggled. She looked at Dream Bunny and said, "I love naps." She jumped down from the big chair to head upstairs. With Dream Bunny tucked under her arm she skipped happily down the upstairs hallway. She stopped abruptly in mid-skip, and whirled around to find both her brother and her sister home from school and close on her heels. Lizzie asked, "Are you gonna scare me again?" They each grabbed one of her arms and pulled her into her bedroom. They all fell into a heap next to Lizzie's bed on the floor. Both Alex and Anna sat crossed legged on the floor, and looked warily back and forth, first at one another and then at Dream Bunny. Anna whispered, "Lizzie, is it true? For real? Those things you said about Dream Bunny?" Lizzie exclaimed in exasperation, "You guys! I keep telling you I went to the place where dreams live and it's the most wonderfulest land you have ever seen!" Not quite convinced, her brother muttered, "I'm not falling for this stuff." Anna looked puzzled and silently pondered what Lizzie had told them. They all stared intently at Dream Bunny, as they sat very still in silence. At that moment no one was aware the door had slowly opened. Mother spoke out, "What are ...." ALL three children SCREAMED.

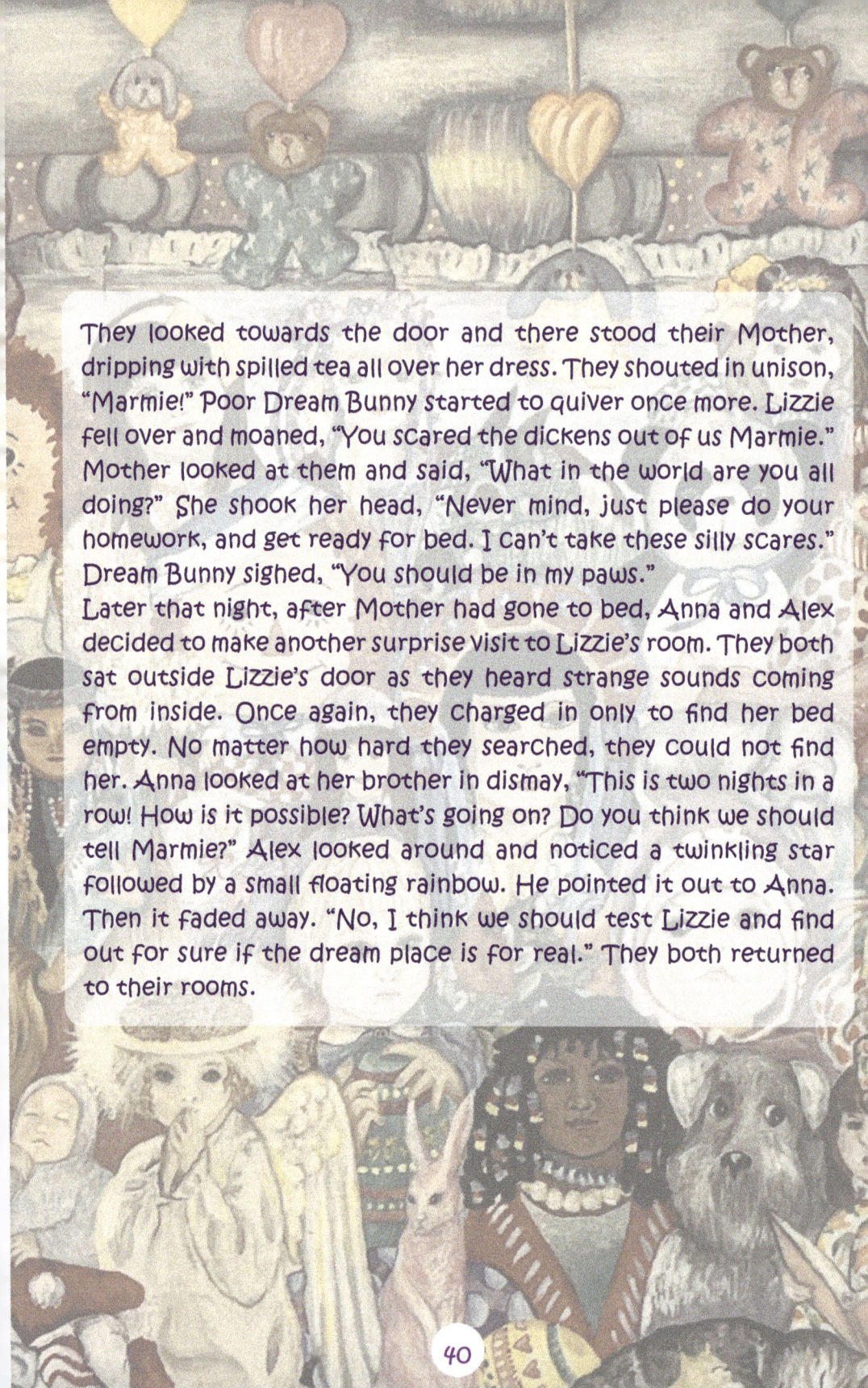

They looked towards the door and there stood their Mother, dripping with spilled tea all over her dress. They shouted in unison, "Marmie!" Poor Dream Bunny started to quiver once more. Lizzie fell over and moaned, "You scared the dickens out of us Marmie." Mother looked at them and said, "What in the world are you all doing?" She shook her head, "Never mind, just please do your homework, and get ready for bed. I can't take these silly scares." Dream Bunny sighed, "You should be in my paws."

Later that night, after Mother had gone to bed, Anna and Alex decided to make another surprise visit to Lizzie's room. They both sat outside Lizzie's door as they heard strange sounds coming from inside. Once again, they charged in only to find her bed empty. No matter how hard they searched, they could not find her. Anna looked at her brother in dismay, "This is two nights in a row! How is it possible? What's going on? Do you think we should tell Marmie?" Alex looked around and noticed a twinkling star followed by a small floating rainbow. He pointed it out to Anna. Then it faded away. "No, I think we should test Lizzie and find out for sure if the dream place is for real." They both returned to their rooms.

TRUE FABLES

The next morning, again a bright light streamed in through the bedroom windows as Lizzie stretched, and opened her eyes. Happy to find herself back in her bed, she giggled to herself. She jumped out of bed, dressed quickly, grabbed Dream Bunny and noticed that Twinkley was still missing. She ran downstairs to have breakfast, swinging Dream Bunny back and forth.

  Mother was in the kitchen fixing breakfast. Lizzie arrived with a big smile, holding Dream Bunny tightly. "Good morning my little angel." Marmie said, as she placed a plate of scrambled eggs on the table for Lizzie. Without warning a rumbling sound came from the stairwell as Alex and Anna ran down full speed trying to be ahead of one another. Alex tripped and fell right in front of Anna. She casually stepped over him, "excuse me," and continued to walk towards the kitchen. Anna sat down first; Alex jumped up on the chair across from Lizzie and stared intently at Lizzie. As Mother placed scrambled eggs in front of Anna and Alex, she asked, "Anna did you finish your homework?" Anna answered, "Yes Marmie." Mother looked over at Alex, "You need a new winter coat. Winter's still upon us, and you have just grown so fast." She looked at all three children who sat in silence, "Okay then, who's for buying an elephant dressed in striped pajamas?" All children answered together. "Okay Marmie." Mother shook her head as she walked out of the kitchen to answer the phone. They continued to glare at Lizzie as she chatted a mile a minute to Dream Bunny.

"I loved the way that puzzle fit together Dream Bunny," Lizzie said, "and the Dream Garden and the Baby Bunny Bugs are sooo cute, and when the Bunny Bees flew. . ." She paused as she turned slowly to look over at Alex and Anna who were staring at her, "What!?" Lizzie questioned. Alex blurted out, "Okay kiddo, where were you hiding?" Anna added, "Alex and I looked everywhere for you last night. Where were you!?" Lizzie, irritated, "I keep telling you! I went to the place of dreams, you silly birds!" Lizzie jumped down from her chair and headed upstairs to her bedroom.

She skipped happily down the upstairs hallway but stopped abruptly in mid-skip, and whirled around to find both her brother and her sister close on her heels. Lizzie demanded, "Don't scare me again!?" Dream Bunny silently agreed, "Please my paws couldn't take it." Again they each grabbed one of her arms and pulled her into the bedroom. They all fell into a heap on her bed. Anna asked in a whisper, "Lizzie, are you sure? Honestly? Those things you said about where dreams live. Is that true?" Lizzie again exasperated, "You guys! I keep telling you I went to this magical place. If I take you with me, will you believe me?" Her siblings nodded their heads excitedly and Lizzie explained to them what they needed to do. Anna skeptically said, "So, what you're saying is this: All we have to do is hold on to Dream Bunny, sink through the covers, sail through the sky of rainbows, and land on fluffy colored clouds. That's it? Then magically we're in the kingdom of dreams?" Lizzie answered, "Uh-huh, and as soon as we're there Dream Bunny will come alive. Then you guys can help me find Twinkley. All we have to do is follow the twinkling stars."

TALES come TRUE

Later that night, Mother quietly made her rounds to give the children a final kiss good night. She first visited Alex's room, but when she opened the door, to her surprise, discovered that not only was he not in his bed, he wasn't even in his room! Next, she looked into Anna's room only to find that her bed was also empty. Finally she headed down the hall to Lizzie's room. To her relief, there, all three were snuggled up together, holding tight to Dream Bunny in Lizzie's bed. Mother held back her laughter as she tipped-toed over to the bed and kissed each one of them good night. Marmie placed a final kiss on Dream Bunny's head and whispered. "Now you take good care of them Dream Bunny, and give them the best dreams for me."

As Mother quietly left the room, the children mumbled drowsily, "G'night, Marmie." As the door closed, the room shimmered with colorful lights, rainbows, swirling stars, and moonbeams. As Mother walked down the stairs, she stopped a moment to look back thinking she heard something, "Oh no Miss Lizzie. You're not going to trick your Marmie." She smiled to herself as she continued her walk down the stairs.

PROMISE of ADVENTURE

Just as Lizzie had said, that very next moment, all three children sank into the quilts. Before they knew it they were floating through the sky and tumbled onto three rainbow slides. Lizzie giggled uncontrollably as she held tightly to Dream Bunny. Anna laughed and shrieked, "Lizzie, how much farther?" They both looked behind to see Alex getting closer. He screamed at the top of his lungs, "YAAAAWWWWHHH!" They were all headed for thousands of multi-colored fluffy clouds.

Falling through the clouds Anna and Lizzie giggled out of control. Alex, on the other hand, continued screaming madly.

PLOP! PLOP! PLOP! All three children landed onto soft puffy clouds.

Dream Bunny hopped up on one of the clouds and welcomed everyone, "Hello! I'm so hoppy you're here!" Anna stuttered, "Oooohhh mmyyy gggooodddness Lllizzzie, yoouur Buunnny tttalks!!!" Lizzie put her hands on her hips, and frowned at Anna, "I told you he did. Why are you surprised?" Twinkley flew up to Alex's nose and twinkled, "Hi Alex. I'm back. How did you like your ride on the rainbow slide?" Alex tripped and fell back over another cloud as he shrieked, "Woooo, a twinkling, talking thingy!" Startled, Twinkley took off again leaving another trail of shining stars.

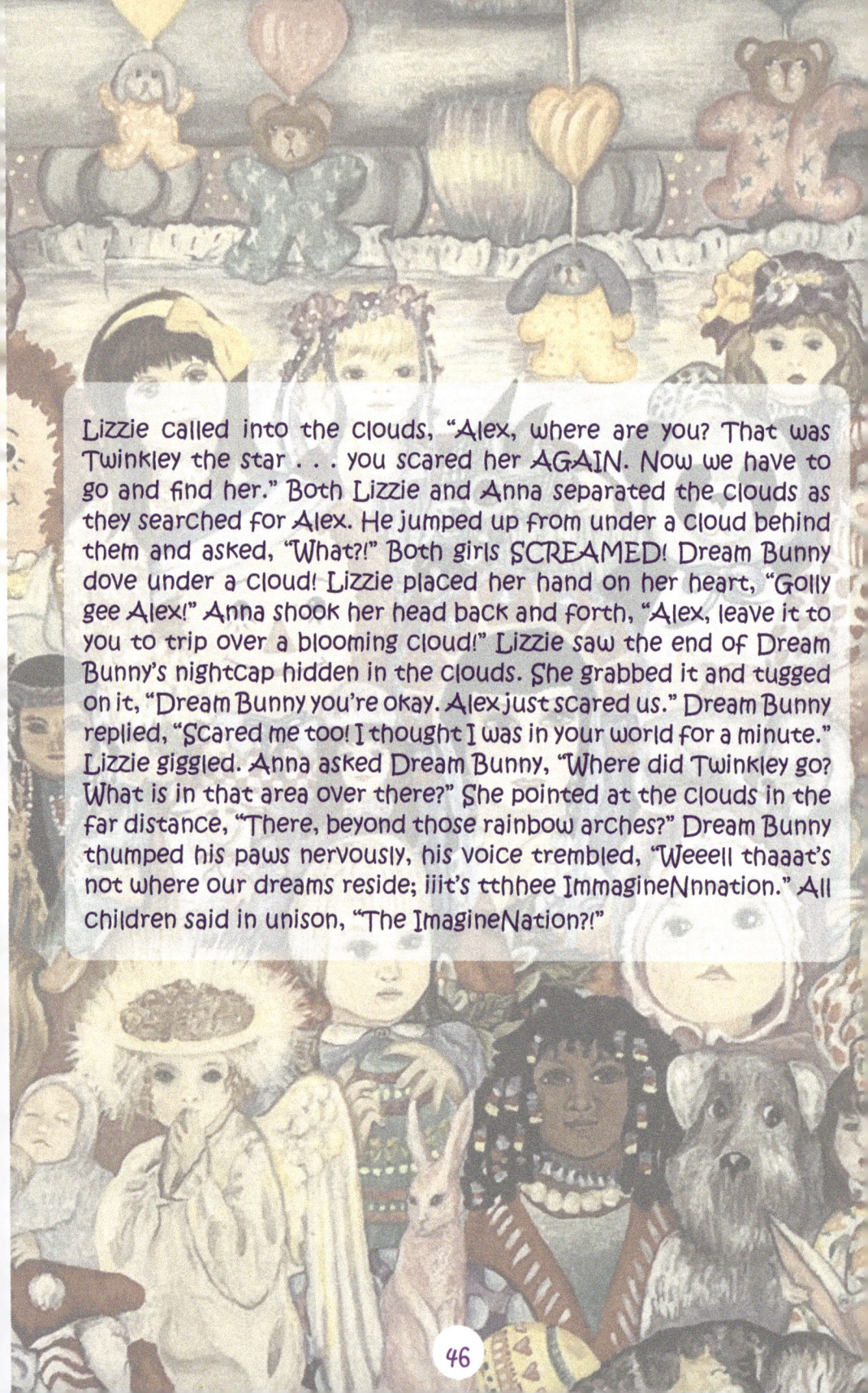

Lizzie called into the clouds, "Alex, where are you? That was Twinkley the star . . . you scared her AGAIN. Now we have to go and find her." Both Lizzie and Anna separated the clouds as they searched for Alex. He jumped up from under a cloud behind them and asked, "What?!" Both girls SCREAMED! Dream Bunny dove under a cloud! Lizzie placed her hand on her heart, "Golly gee Alex!" Anna shook her head back and forth, "Alex, leave it to you to trip over a blooming cloud!" Lizzie saw the end of Dream Bunny's nightcap hidden in the clouds. She grabbed it and tugged on it, "Dream Bunny you're okay. Alex just scared us." Dream Bunny replied, "Scared me too! I thought I was in your world for a minute." Lizzie giggled. Anna asked Dream Bunny, "Where did Twinkley go? What is in that area over there?" She pointed at the clouds in the far distance, "There, beyond those rainbow arches?" Dream Bunny thumped his paws nervously, his voice trembled, "Weeell thaaat's not where our dreams reside; iiit's tthhee ImmagineNnnation." All children said in unison, "The ImagineNation?!"

NOTION of a NATION

Dream Bunny and the children cautiously walked across the meadow reaching the entrance through the rainbow arches. They looked through the archway and the path of twinkling stars as they entered into a dark and gloomy trail. Lizzie took a deep breath, "Dream Bunny, are you sure we have to go in?" Dream Bunny nervously nodded, "Yes it's the only way we can find her." They all walked towards a place that looked like a city, sculpted out of a huge solid gloomy cloud beyond another enormous rainbow tree. Anna pointed to the ground and said, "Look everyone, let's follow those twinkling stars through the clouds." When they reached the rainbow trees, the path of stars went into two different directions. Lizzie looked over at Dream Bunny, and asked, "Which way do we go?" Alex started to spit in his palm . . . Anna stopped him, "Oh no you don't; we go that way!" Anna pointed to the left.

As they walked through the forest of rainbow trees everything seemed cheerful except the occasional puff of gray clouds blocking their sight. They stuck close to each other as the once delightful soft music turned into spooky sounds of haunted echoes in the place called the ImagineNation. Anna, Alex, Lizzie, and Dream Bunny continued to tippy toe very slowly as they moved on. Alex spoke out, "Hey!" Everyone SCREAMED. Dream Bunny hopped into Lizzie's arms and Lizzie jumped into Anna's arms, all falling to the ground. Alex started to laugh, "You guys, quit foolin' around." Dream Bunny started to quiver, shake and stutter, "Alex, dddon't say thaat!" Lizzie asked, "What? Foolin'...?" Dream Bunny put his paw on Lizzie's mouth and whispered, "Be careful, the fooleries will hear you." Alex leaned in real close and whispered, "I was just going to ask," he huffed, "where did all the toys go?"

IMAGINE THAT?

Dream Bunny held tight to Lizzie's hand while Anna and Alex walked ahead of them. They stepped cautiously as they kept their eyes on the sparkling trail of stars beneath them. The clouds became a little darker as they continued to walk. Then they began to march, trying to show confidence and looked back only to realize the joyful music in the distance from their kingdom of dreams was fading.

Alex started to skip, and then he began to whistle. Lizzie held tight to Dream Bunny. Anna stopped and hushed Alex. He looked back, "What?" Anna with her hands on her hips, glared at him, then she stomped her foot at him, "Is it too much to ask you to be quiet for a few minutes?" As Anna turned to walk away, Alex stuck his tongue out at her and began to whistle louder. Lizzie showed frustration and said, "Alex, what's that song?" Alex smiled, and replied, "Marmie's favorite. "Daisy, Daisy. . ."

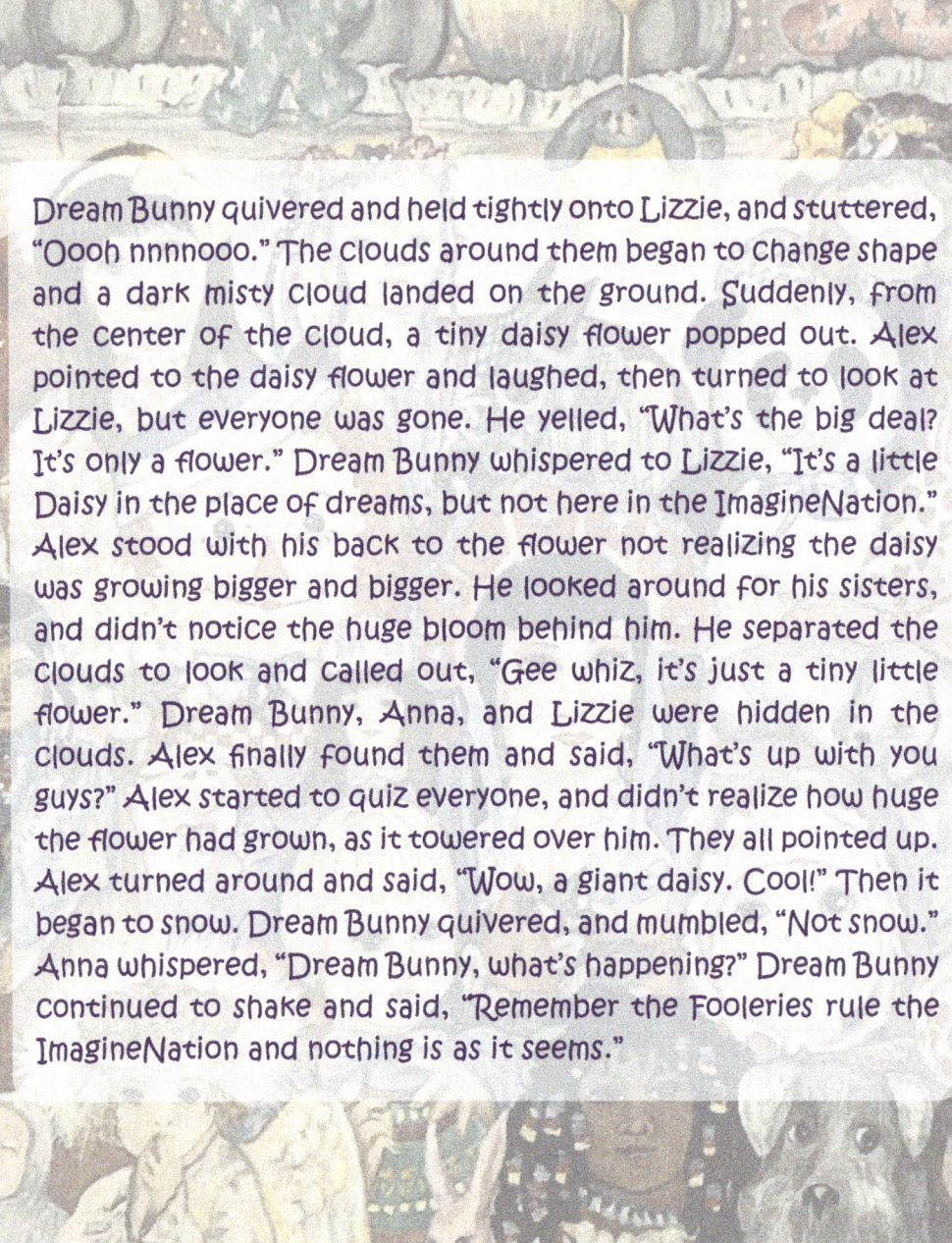

Dream Bunny quivered and held tightly onto Lizzie, and stuttered, "Oooh nnnnooo." The clouds around them began to change shape and a dark misty cloud landed on the ground. Suddenly, from the center of the cloud, a tiny daisy flower popped out. Alex pointed to the daisy flower and laughed, then turned to look at Lizzie, but everyone was gone. He yelled, "What's the big deal? It's only a flower." Dream Bunny whispered to Lizzie, "It's a little Daisy in the place of dreams, but not here in the ImagineNation." Alex stood with his back to the flower not realizing the daisy was growing bigger and bigger. He looked around for his sisters, and didn't notice the huge bloom behind him. He separated the clouds to look and called out, "Gee whiz, it's just a tiny little flower." Dream Bunny, Anna, and Lizzie were hidden in the clouds. Alex finally found them and said, "What's up with you guys?" Alex started to quiz everyone, and didn't realize how huge the flower had grown, as it towered over him. They all pointed up. Alex turned around and said, "Wow, a giant daisy. Cool!" Then it began to snow. Dream Bunny quivered, and mumbled, "Not snow." Anna whispered, "Dream Bunny, what's happening?" Dream Bunny continued to shake and said, "Remember the Fooleries rule the ImagineNation and nothing is as it seems."

WORDS come ALIVE

The storm grew stronger and the snow began to get heavier and heavier. Dream Bunny looked up as snow fell on his face, "Seriously?" Daisy got bigger and bigger, and the ground below her started to loosen. The children stared in disbelief as Daisy found a way to get loose from the ground, and stomped towards them. Her feet were huge roots and she had an enormous mouth and spoke in a deep voice. She slowly said, "Where are you at, my Little Morsels?" Lizzie whispered, "What's a morsel?" Dream Bunny started to tremble, and uttered, "Fooood." The snow got stronger and the huge flower found the children and Dream Bunny, even though they tried to hide in the clouds. In a deep voice, Daisy bellowed, "There you are!" Alex screamed, "Run!" They all ran in and under the gray clouds. The storm got heavier, and the wind started to blow and the giant Daisy got closer and closer. The children started to shiver. Lizzie said, "It's like our world, cold and icy." Dream Bunny shook, and said mockingly, "I know." Daisy suddenly froze, as snow and icicles covered every inch of the giant's bloom. Anna looked up just at that moment to see Daisy bend down over them. Daisy said, with a thundering voice, "Snacks!" They all SCREAMED. . . "Ooohh NOOO!"
As Daisy leaned over, her giant mouth opened, she snapped at the children, but fortunately the movement caused the frozen flower to shatter into a flurry of snowflakes. Dream Bunny looked up, and as the snow fell on his face, he sighed, "I now love snow."

THAT HAPPENED

As the children and Dream Bunny walked slowly through the clouds and melted snow, Alex started to speak, "Where...?" They all hushed him. Alex showed frustration and said, "Hey, things turned out okay!" They turned and all stared at Alex at the same time. Anna went nose to nose with him, frustrated, and said, "You have got to be kidding me?" Lizzie looked over at Dream Bunny, and said in a soft voice, "Hope they're saying something nice to each other!" Dream Bunny replied, "Me too." Alex and Anna continued to stare each other down, then Alex spoke very loud, "Why do I always get the blame?" Anna turned and retorted, "I know we are all supposed to get along, but it just bugs me at times . . ." Dream Bunny quickly turned his head to look at Lizzie, and said, "Oh no, here we go again." Lizzie's eyes got huge, and then she whispered, "What do you mean?"

From a distance they heard a buzzing sound. It got louder and louder. Three tiny Bunny Bees flew up to Anna and Alex's faces. Lizzie pointed and said, "Look Dream Bunny, it's okay. They're cute little Baby Bunny Bees from the garden."

Dream Bunny shook, and mumbled, "Remember Lizzie this is not our magical place."

Anna forced a laugh, "See no big deal", she gulped, "cute Baby Bunny Bees." Dream Bunny covered his eyes. Lizzie said, "Oh no, that's bad, huh?" Dream Bunny nodded, yes.

The Baby Bunny Bees started to grow larger and larger until they were the size of three large buses. The buzzing sounded like thunder and they all screamed as they all ran.

Terrified, they ran through the area of the melted snow. Looking across the field they finally got close to a clearing of an open meadow totally exhausted.

Dream Bunny pointed across the area and said, "Look, rainbow arches!" Suddenly the thunder sound got louder and closer. Alex screamed, "What good are rainbow arches?" Dream Bunny replied, "They can't go through that archway to our peaceful kingdom." Anna turned and saw the giant Bunny Bees coming straight for them. She shrieked, "Ruuuuun!"

As they ran, Alex looked over at Anna and yelled, "This time it's not my fault!" As they reached the rainbow archway, they all dove through the arches to cross into the kingdom of dreams. The giant Bunny Bees hit the Rainbow Arches and disappeared. Everyone rolled to the ground exhausted and grateful.

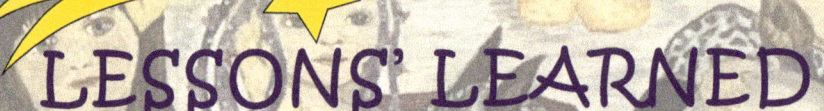
LESSONS' LEARNED

Suddenly, a bright light appeared, and as the children looked up, they all shouted, "Twinkley!" She sparkled up to each one of them and twinkled, "How did you like your wonderful adventure?"
Anna frowned and replied, "You have got to be kidding. It was horrible!" Alex piped in, "Why did you lead us down the wrong path? It was no dream. It was a nightmare!" Twinkley twinkled up to Alex's nose. "It was the right path." All the children said together, "The right path!?" Dream Bunny giggled, "Twinkley is right. When you all went into the ImagineNation, what did you all learn?" Lizzie exclaimed, "I know, I know! We learned to stick together." Dream Bunny giggled. Then Alex said, "Also, words are real!" Everyone laughed. Anna said, "To know that we all make mistakes and not to blame others."
Then the Bunny Butterflies, Baby Bunny Bees, and lots of toys came into the garden and cheered, "Yay to our new friends Alex, Anna, and Lizzie!" Everyone laughed and fell back on the rainbow grass.
Twinkley sparkled brightly over the children and sprinkled stardust on them. They all closed their eyes and fell asleep.

BUNNIES n' more BUNNIES

Lizzie's eyes were tightly shut as she cuddled Dream Bunny in her arms. A bright beam of light shone through her bedroom window once more. She stretched and blinked her eyes, and said, "Dream Bunny that was the bestest adventure ever!" She then grabbed Dream Bunny's nightcap and found Twinkley dangling at the end. She giggled, "You're back! Yippee!"

The door burst open, Anna and Alex jumped up and down, and Lizzie screamed, and then giggled. They all held up a Dream Bunny and said together, "Look Dream Bunny!" Lizzie whispered, "How could that be?" Everyone sat on the bed and looked at each other while they examined their new found friends. Lizzie exclaimed, "But look, only one Twinkley." A twinkle sound was heard and they all laughed. Alex said, "We heard anything's possible." They all smiled at each other. Anna asked the others, "Why do you think there are three Dream Bunny toys?" Lizzie took a deep breath, "What if there are thousands?" They all fell back on the bed and smiled as they each held their own Dream Bunny.

Mother walked down the hallway, but this time she was with her sister Susan, who was Mary's younger sister. Mary turned to her sister, "Better warn them we're coming in." Susan looked at her puzzled. "I'll explain later." Susan had two young children of her own, (seven year old twins), Mason her son, and his sister Brooklyn. Mason was the explorer and Brooklyn was a bookworm with an imagination like Lizzie. Mary said, "Surprise! Look who's here?" Susan stepped out from behind the door. The children all cheered, "Auntie!"

Without warning, in burst their cousins, Mason and Brooklyn holding up their new found Dream Bunnies. Mason blurted out,

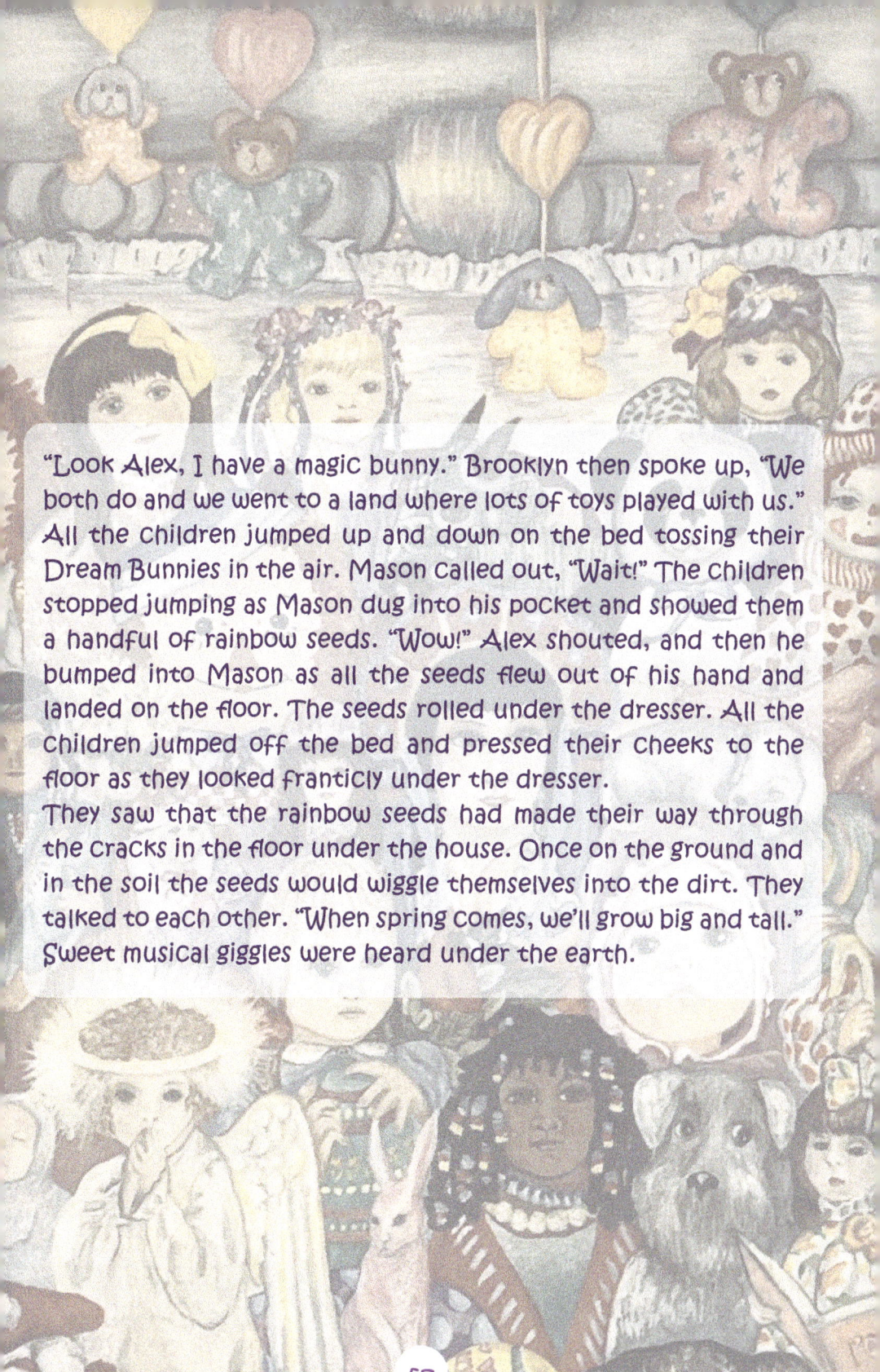

"Look Alex, I have a magic bunny." Brooklyn then spoke up, "We both do and we went to a land where lots of toys played with us." All the children jumped up and down on the bed tossing their Dream Bunnies in the air. Mason called out, "Wait!" The children stopped jumping as Mason dug into his pocket and showed them a handful of rainbow seeds. "Wow!" Alex shouted, and then he bumped into Mason as all the seeds flew out of his hand and landed on the floor. The seeds rolled under the dresser. All the children jumped off the bed and pressed their cheeks to the floor as they looked frantically under the dresser.

They saw that the rainbow seeds had made their way through the cracks in the floor under the house. Once on the ground and in the soil the seeds would wiggle themselves into the dirt. They talked to each other. "When spring comes, we'll grow big and tall." Sweet musical giggles were heard under the earth.

ANYTHING is POSSIBLE

Anna glared at Alex. "Seriously. . ." Brooklyn asked Lizzie, "are they always like that?" Lizzie answers, "You have no idea."
 Lizzie quietly said, "Maybe they'll come back as rainbow flowers when the snow goes away."
 "Anything is possible, even in the real world." Twinkley chimed as loud as she could. This time all the children understood her and giggled. With all the possible new adventures they all laughed and cheered as they held tight to their Dream Bunnies.
Knowing anything is possible, children from all over the world can find their way to the Place of Dreams, and on occasion visit the ImagineNation to learn a different kind of lesson; which gives every child an adventure they will never forget.

   Remember, Sweet Dreams to A Happily Ever After

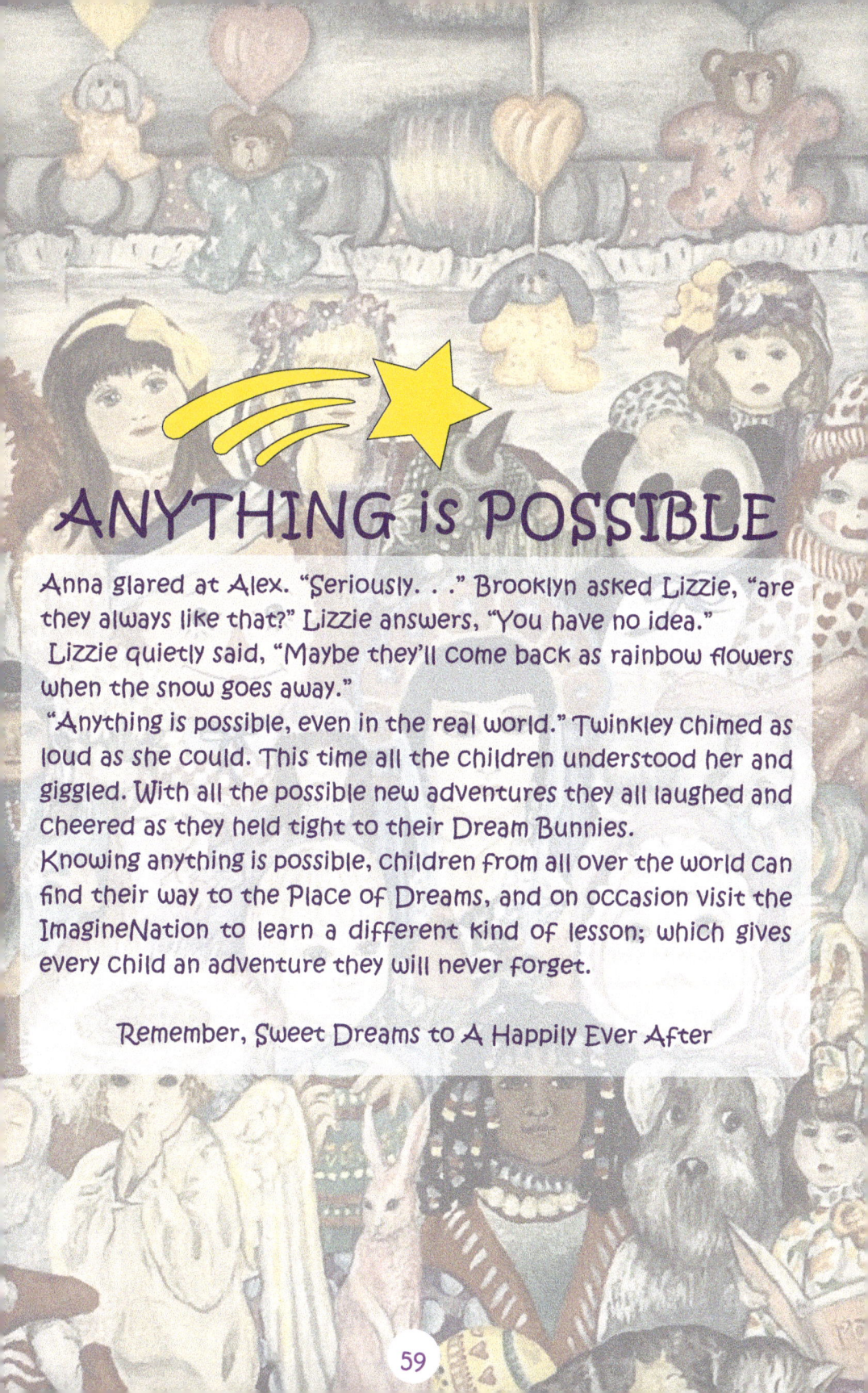

10620 Treena Street, Suite 230
San Diego, California,
CA 92131 USA
www.readersmagnet.com
1.619.354.2643
Copyright 2022 All Rights Reserved

www.ingramcontent.com/pod-product-compliance
Lightning Source LLC
LaVergne TN
LVHW050137080526
838202LV00061B/6509